ANNA'S GAME!

by Anne Phillips
illustrated by Denise and Fernando

Scott Foresman

Editorial Offices: Glenview, Illinois • New York, New York
Sales Offices: Reading, Massachusetts • Duluth, Georgia
Glenview, Illinois • Carrollton, Texas • Menlo Park, California

Anna loved to play baseball.
"Throw the ball!" said Ben.
Anna threw the ball. But she
threw it the wrong way.

Anna loved to play football.
"Run with the ball!" said Maya.
Anna ran with the ball. But she ran the wrong way.

Anna loved to play soccer.
"Kick the ball!" said James.
Anna kicked the ball. But she
kicked it the wrong way.

Anna still loves to play ball. Sometimes Anna plays another game. Then she has lots of company. She and her friends play "Anna Ball." They have so much fun.

You can kick the ball. You can throw the ball. Then you can run with the ball. You can do anything with the ball. This game does not have any rules.

The score is zero to zero. Or it is forty to forty. Or it is one million to one million.

And everybody wins!